ADVANCE P
M

"Loosely based on Hesiod's Theogeny, Maxwell I. Gold's anOther Mythology deconstructs traditional mythic narratives and tropes in a defiantly transgressive take on cosmic origin stories. Indeed, the Muses must have conferred Hesiod's kingly scepter of authority to Gold, and he uses it wisely. Gold fearlessly flings open closet doors, unveils dark deceptions, and reshapes the cosmos to unshackle the stars. A stunning reclamation of Greek myth."

—Carina Bissett, award-winning editor of *Shadow Atlas: Dark Landscapes of the Americas*

"Maxwell I. Gold's poetry pulls from the heart and bleeds truth onto the page."

—Michael Bailey, multi-award-winning author and editor.

ANOTHER MYTHOLOGY

Poems

MAXWELL I. GOLD

ANOTHER MYTHOLOGY

Text Copyright © 2023 by Maxwell I. Gold

Cover art by Dan Sauers.

Edited by Holly Lyn Walrath.

Published by Interstellar Flight Press

Houston, Texas.

www.interstellarflightpress.com

ISBN (eBook): 978-1-953736-25-3

ISBN (Paperback): 978-1-953736-24-6

CONTENTS

ANOTHER MYTHOLOGY

anOther Theogony, anOther Mythology

The story never ends. The System came, another god forged in the light of a new universe, nameless to its worshippers but all-too recognizable in the awful cruelties, the normative chains which pulled down beast and god alike as Displacement and Other were soon birthed from that which was unmistakable.

Displacement followed, the System's progeny, another child of that wretched pantheon pushed through their wide jaws, the inequitable distribution of life, light, and fear across existence where emerged from their blood, Paranoia, the long-haired wretch too naïve and ashamed to leave his closet—and Fear, the leathery serpent-boy who slunk across the dark musty innards betwixt star and broken dreams of the universe, danced atop crumbs of dread, forever smeared beneath him.

The children of the System were too numerous to count —the worst of these Fear, Displacement, and Confinement, the spoiled brat who swallowed hope and Light so easily into the pits and impractical depths never to peer beyond his lips. Of course, many more followed, and their names were inconsequential compared to the destructions wrought by their respective siblings and the System's hunger.

Most pitiful, forgotten by the rest, especially the System, was the Other, a bastard some said, never meant to be and pushed aside into the darkest closets of the universe when the high walls of their confinement were torn asunder. The Other stood taller and more imposing than the stars, anomalous and beautiful, and ripped the ancient chains from the cracked foundations as the System fell, piece by piece. So the story continued, and the System went, another nameless god forgotten to the Other.

False Expectations

Expectations screw with perceptions of light, fantasy, even blood and bone. They certainly did mine. Gods, monsters, and all the contemptible soap operas bellowed the same betrayals and mundane problems. Maybe that was the drag, not me. Things had to change, and luckily, I had it all worked out. Myths cooked in marble pots penned the conceptions where divinities poured down from white-nimbus castles in tender clothed and ivory-skinned gods, but lies were the song of history and myth perpetuated erroneous what-ifs and god-smacked blasphemies.

So too, the stories were passed down, and perhaps I'd weave myself into the legend, throwing the twisted metal of expectation into the hot, gurgling forges where word and reason might re-write and reshape that which sought to contort the pantheons of yesterday into some jaded, wretched theogony.

I am Death
(Thanatos' Arrogance)

Flashes, spectral ambivalence, and guttural music orchestrated in the last pitiful moments before the body fades into memory. They'll never forget me. I can't help myself, or the dramatics, but I've been taught not to play with my food. Bodies, brain, and beautiful dreams coalesce my hunger until nothing remains for me to do except swallow everything into the darkness of my forgotten stomach, where fingers lick the salt and stars, only wanting

one

more

bite. Too much?

He'll survive, he always has beneath that helmet . . . at least I think he will, if I don't finish everyone, everything off, first bit by bit, down to the last atom, I really can't help myself, though it's difficult to hold back the urge to swallow and take

one

more

bite, from the lights, the gods,

and stars.

I am Dead
(Hades' Plea)

They always forget me, the Closet of Shadows. I'm here in the shadows, too, a host for those poor unfortunates always terrified without cause, without anything, and too quick to make the jump or the last kiss when they're brought to me in this place of dark cavernous dreams and helmets taller than their nightmares.

They

Always

Forget,

I've been here for countless millennia, waiting, watching, witness to the birth of stars though forever misunderstood and still stranded in my own closet of shadows. Doomed to care for these wild unfortunates who glide through *His* lips, *His* sloppy seconds.

And they always forget, but I remain here, in this closet of shadows.

Post-Eros

Wading inside the sticky, glittery, globulous mass that was the Night before the others; before the Abyss in his bottomless hunger; before Chaos and her cantankerous, jagged temper; before the rock and wrath that was Earth; I sat content in imperceptible Voids manipulating emotion, bleeding with rage and destiny. The crackle of new stars and wild myths, engendered by the tantalizing spark of *what-if* spurred billions toward my love. That was the way of it—the truth of things, despite the false destinies and designs constructed to gaslight my reality.

Still, the curse of longing persisted through the ages and would forever burn inside me; after the Abyss found that final destruction which consumed him and all his debaucheries pleasure; after Chaos was twisted inside out from unending cycles of entropy, blasting away the remnants of beauty, bone, and atom; after the pitiful rock was sucked dry entirely of life and thought, only the emotionless beasts which roamed the metal sphere in a black web of nothingness; and I was left happy, swollen with completeness, love, and never-again.

No Gods, No Sea Beneath the Waves

There were no gods, monsters, or demons beneath the ocean swells, only black faces, clever tricks to avoid the crushing depths, and despicable, foamy darkness. I was no different than those who came before me—carved in marble, those laughing facades drowned in washed-up philosophies as pretend masters of the sea. They were faulty manipulations carved in salt and scorched brains, pulsing through the ages until another one of us was crushed or cursed by the seas. I, too, was a mutant realized, in the chain unbroken, as the waters whispered treasonous thoughts, preparing to slit the throats of those who thought themselves the false gods of the waters of the universe.

Bubbles less numerous and air pockets as rare as gemstones as the darkness crept in through the ruins and wrath of sunken worlds—and my ability to think, to breathe, became more like some flash-bang dream. My time was coming to a close, and there soon would be another to replace the false pretenders of the sea.

The Moth

I was many things to many universes and civilizations. Perhaps a dragon or beast, some winged gemstone-carrying behemoth who dwelled at the center of existence, the personification of earthquakes, or a force so great the fabrics of reality ripped beneath my bulk.

So large even that my body altered perceptions and dreams wherever I moved, pulling the stars across my sparkling mass over timelines and twisted cyber-structures as if they were twine caught in my fingers. Over and under, through swirling fire-pits and graveyards of shadows, floating in the darkness, cradled in the nightmares of every living organism, I grew to become the infinite dread-many, in name and form. Names carved in ink, blood, and dark curses failed to discern the nature of my hideous scale.

I was many things to many universes and civilizations, or perhaps a dragon or beast, but always *Moth*.

Croesus' Coin

I saw borders spread toward the end of the world beneath the glint and glare of golden eyes whose metallic fingers clutched the hulking mass of Earth as if to pull it deeper inside himself, the old king, away from the prying eyes of the world. Surveying a kingdom cleaved entirely from flesh, freedom, and purity of light, the colossus bestrode me with basalt columns and granite eyes peering into my soul where he found the missing piece of his metal heart.

Minted in the earthly bowels unreachable by human hands, he pulled apart cities, mountains, and cut down fortunes by unfulfilled desires to claw at the molten depths where he found me, compressed in rock and ruin, the price of his primal and kingly conquest, though never truly his. Pulled closer unto his breast, coveted and concealed from the glare of modernity; I slept forever with the bones of a sad, lonely king.

Across the Seas, Into the Desert
I'd Have You Again

I never meant for it to come to this—to see you in such a condition, never meant to wander endless eons to see that corpse once more, which was always mine. Long ago, in my wildest and darkest dreams, I saw your body plucked from crystal waters, wrapped in chains deep inside some closet-casket where I searched frantically across the ages through the Old Kingdoms now swallowed in sand and death, forgotten to the world— you forgotten by the world, but never by me—never again.

Bloodied and bruised by the gods so jealous, hateful of our forbidden passions, they ripped your kiss from my tired lips where the music and stars created from my baleful lamentations rose towards that most beautiful, rubescent sunset cradled between ancient ruin—longing for a familiar touch, a reminder I'd cross the seas, traverse the cosmic sands if it meant I'd hold you again.

Where Roots Run Deep

i.

Across the seas where roots run deep and strange, creatures without tongues and covered in soot and powder slunk beneath a starless night. In the deserts and woods of the Old World, the dead walked with open mouths, ready to gorge on sweet, tender, pale flesh.

We were the hierophants, cursed and shamed by systemic cruelties, reclaimed by bokor talismans and ancestors who needed us.

We were the bodies of yellow stars and old trees, corpses left to be buried but risen once more to feast in shadow and sand, to laugh in voiceless tones as the bloody ebullience of tomorrow covered our lips,

ii.

Where roots run deep, across the seas, into the Night, footsteps crushed upturned sprigs, the Gods ran from their undead guilt, a hunger unmistakable dressed in the bones and ink of burnt flesh, rusted skin, and dancing skulls in the Night that was indifferent to flesh, and the arbiter of souls no matter

the lies or stories told about us,

the Hoods who'd never burn or bury us, Crimson Faced Things who dug graves in the catacombs of pragmatic and perverse, and the Old World soon died

> Where roots
> run deep.

iii.

The truth was buried within the womb of the Earth, sealed by bone and broken histories never told until the trees themselves, felled by hateful Crimson, once again disturbing the Earth and the things that move, stirring in the dirt and dank unspoken peripheries of cream-colored guilty-gods who fear the gnawing of teeth and the ripped flesh which stinks and stains the inside of stolen temples, fled across the seas.

Phobos Oneiroi:
Into the Mouth of Fear

Too late, I followed the ruined road where not even Jupiter dared to tread. Beneath white stars as titans slept, I saw an ancient mouth agape, begging me to step closer inside the endless dark. Bone and rock, like crooked teeth protruded from the lazy, twisted door to Erebus' lonely, desolate kingdom. My legs felt paralyzed at the sight of something covered in dread and misery, yet, muscle and flesh overpowered any sense I had as I lumbered through the Gates of Oblivion

deeper,

farther,

into Lethe's cruel, forgetful embrace, awash in a warm, unnerving spectral embrace as if the stars themselves were slowly going out around me, drying up, my thirst unquenchable until sorrow was everywhere as heavy as the Gem of Sisyphus being pushed

higher,

farther,

toward the vast eyes of Acheron, filled with immense disappointment equivalent to the scorn of a thousand rusted knives—it was unbearable, and there was nothing to release me from this cosmic paresthesia. Soon, the cold and metallic bled away into light, flame, and laughter as I free-fell

deeper,

faster,

without any a sense of time or care into the whirling liquescence of hatred, like Phlegethon's molten fingertips, where gods themselves trembled, afraid of that which awaited them, awaiting me within the stone belly of the world. When, too late, I followed that ruined road not even Jupiter dared to tread.

Endymion the Twink and the Vengeful Moon

Pressed against the flesh of night glared the eyes of the jealous Moon, too hungry to see past his own stare; the ivory skin and dimpled cheeks of the boy laid on the nameless mountainside. Unaware and blissful, the youth cared not for the will wrought by pallid gods and rotten stars, lusting for the skin of yesterday with only the hope of tomorrow; he refused the advances from the terrible Moon.

Night after gloom-filled night, the amber glint from above grew worse, and the calls more raucous in musical derangement like some twisted symphony, whose orchestrations were composed by mad-obstruent noises, where the grass and trees smacked o'er the rocks as if to mutilate all sense of silence and calm.

Refuse me not! Compelled the Moon, through tired, ancient eyes, although the naïve boy continued to lie on the mountainside amid the thunderous cackle and ruinous frustrations which grew above him.

Refuse me not, arrogant youth! The stars trembled while the horrid moon bled light and lust from its rocky innards across the valleys, through the forests until no light was seen from any city or palace except the corpse of the old god, which hung dimly in the fabric of night, and the nameless boy who slept forever on the mountainside without knowing anything of the Moon.

Anti-Orpheus:
The Music of Death

Through the burning gates of Hell, clutched against my breast, he was mine to have; no matter the awful bargains struck by wretched plutonian god-kings. How I longed for his touch, but too heavy was the music of darksome lullabies which pulled down the stars themselves into loathsome, blissful oblivion. Sprayed across the saggy horizon sounded my infinite chorus of bemused longing for the one whose soul-corpse, carried in my hands, was never truly mine again.

Drown

    beneath my heavy,

        sorrowful tears.

Drown.

I blasted deep through the soil, and every blade of grass trembled in grief and fear as trees felled without a crack of the wind over hills and villages that never understood, though they cried out in dread at my deathful songs. It wasn't enough for them, for what they took away from me, louder and vengeful, I played through the heavens as the very night crawled back towards their palace at the edge of the darkness, but it wasn't far enough to escape my tears. No one would escape.

Drown

    beneath my heavy,

                sorrowful tears.

Drown.

The Clay and Cruel, The Prometheus

Designs sculpted in blood, bone, and mud walked the sullen Earth without repose, manacled by a grim fate and folly prescribed only to dimwitted gods, content with the high-level conscription of stars, whose fire and fantasy pulled down gods without consent and twisted into a mutilated species.

Prepared to spread over reality, these putrid automatons waltzed through the emptiness, hungry and hopeful. Perhaps there was an answer to their misshapen, misgendered existence. Never given the opportunity to understand the flames which bellowed inside the cold, constricted tissue, never malleable enough to conform to the wild, defamed pantheons whose moralities laughed, *never good enough* or *fall back into place.*

No, they stole the fire gifted by heathen deities who professed to know better to reshape what they didn't understand; and destroy the temples, cities, and alters in the name of that horrid Prometheus.

Pangu, the Anti-King

Two sides of the same halves, confined to an egg for eighteen-thousand years, where the same story weaved endlessly throughout history—the false expectation of my identity, limbs, brains, body, heart, and mind seed and sanctuary for those who desired only justification for an existence which was meaningless. Flesh to dirt, blood to water, brain to sky—the awful fertilization and broken dreams left me without beauty or choice.

Closet doors like temples built at the altar of my hallowed bones, erected in the foggy nights, swung wide when finally the shell cracked slightly for the world to understand, past the hills softened by faded muscle, the decayed perfumes in sad fields like oxidized fluids, and the forests cut down from what remained of my fragile hairs, laid bare to the eyes of the ignorant, was me, the Anti-King.

Below, The Pit

Below the skies, and farther still, haunting those bewildered spaces where tiny cracks formed at the fork of maybe-so, on the banks of trembling rivers at the base of unformed nightmares, I waited in the Pits cleaved from black and brittle sanguinity. A glass-blown geography of the horrid flames of yesterday glazed across a plain that once had woods but now held only deserts and mountains cut down into oceans of jagged diamonds and rocks bleeding into the bodies of five rivers.

Those siblings of mine, too few left, tried to confine me. They threw scraps into my ash-fired stomach to quell the ancient resentment which boiled deep, past the gray glutted clouds into the whirling smog, where my hatred seethed as if buried in some unnatural closet. Forgotten to the minds and memories of comprehension, forgotten to the gods and my vile siblings, I toiled below the skies and farther still in a place confined to the primordial atrocities of creations—the empty, forsaken Pit of Tartarus.

I Am Yawn

Always, forever, and into the wide infinite darkness, I stretched my lips towards that which never ended, my unyielding loneliness. I was, and had always been, the voids. Even Tartarus trembled when gazing into my heavy depths or the nightmares creeping far beneath visions not even the Fates dared to utter, or the Graeae whispered in the foggy, black murk of their rocky palaces at the edge of death and wonder. No, nothing compared to my thirst for solitude and contempt for order as if it were possible to truly subdue me or the powers that tugged at the bodies of the cosmos.

The pitiful attempts at naming me were also fruitless and humorful: Chaos, Primordial, The Beginning . . . though there was something simpler to describe it.

Dreadful and unsettling.

Wider my lips parted through the darkness, and I managed to draw a single breath. A billion lights flickered in and out of existence, countless pains insinuated but never felt, and even gods were lost to me.

I am Yawn.

Blood and Flowers:
Saffron Nightmares

Those golden fields of wheat and memory were littered
with purple bulbs whose red fingertips tickled the
heartless wind; longing for the touch of flesh once more.
Taken from the solemnity of flesh, ne'er granted peace by
the gods, those flowers that once were flesh of man could
no longer bear the embrace of a love forbidden in a world
othered by their queer and confused passions. Not even
the darkest chthonic sanctuaries welcomed them, nor
their unions, which many, even the gods, considered
unholy, despite the unbreakable love which bonded them
together as if forged in the belly of stars.

Deep, throbbing, and unending.

The pain was too great a burden to shoulder, so the
mortal begged his life be taken away if he could not be? in
the hands of that love which burned hotter than the
eldest of Voids. Still, the Gods denied him, pushed him
towards closeted darkness, and when Death, too, denied
him the peace owed to a heartbroken like a billion shards
of glass sought strange and dark magics to free himself
from the existence that chained him to that wretched
Earth. Through dim and shadowed night, he traveled
across nameless plains, beneath mountains and madness;
until he happened upon a golden field said to have

belonged to an ancient god, unimportant in name and stature, who was cast out by their kin.

Relieve me of this burden, he beseeched the old god, but the god said nothing, save a dark and terrible warning crooned from the god's lips, *Here you shall remain, if you choose; the blood and flowers left behind, bound in grief no more.*

And so, the man remained forever within the golden fields of wheat and memory, littered with purple bulbs whose red fingertips tickled the heartless wind, longing for the touch of flesh once more, never to have or hold it again.

The Fall of Cin

Conceived beneath the lust of stars inside the flesh forges, hidden away for the pleasure of the Sun-God himself, the most beautiful thing emerged through amniotic metal and molten desires. The ivory and broad-shouldered figure stood taller than any mortal man, causing jealousy and derisive confrontation that reached even the Gods and Stars. So much so, no manner of hiding could stay the rage that pulled the Sun from his horizon where Night embraced the beauty and warmth of the clay man known to the world as Cin.

No god resisted the alluring charm, and even the ancient Night, with all its shadow and darksome terror, fell limp under the grasp of Cin, who'd grown callous and hungry for more. When the deep, churning skies were no longer enough to control his appetites, Cin had grown bored of the Night and moved onward to greater conquests; the Seas which proved ne'er a challenge; the Voids ne'er deep enough, and the Stars ne'er bright enough.

Still, the Sun-God stewed in his palace of light and flame, enraged by the lustful monster let loose on the world. In his own wrath and jealousy, the Sun-God screamed with fire and hatred; a light so great to burn the oceans; to scorch the shadows themselves; to destroy the stars so that Cin might be starved of love and devotion.

The Tree of Other
(The Other Tree)

These roots ran deep, deep into the heart of the world—beneath the waters and ruin of the heartless flesh-things who crawled on the surface and through the darkest crevices in the night—existing before the Voids or vague shadows floating across the bloated, plastic fields, spreading like an ivory bile on the world.

I'd been called many names in the time before; Home, Monster, Beautiful, or Bitch, but no matter the derisive mythologies painted and carved into my body, I remained. Scarred, slandered, and stayed throughout the star-cut ages, I dug deeper into the decay filling the moments with beauty and purpose, despite the awful anxieties which threatened to rip my foundations.

When the cities and stars grew darker, silent in the majesty of Death and Time, only then did the names and treasons carved in my skin feel as if they were the only comfort in a truly empty universe, where my roots run deep, forever into the heart of existence.

The Graveyard of the Gods

I saw this place where gods die, on an island at the center of the universe. Surrounded by earth, trees, and the liquesecent blood of the planet where life was cradled against the crystalline inlets, dancing sugar palms, and wide-eyed banyam trees, I knew this was both the beginning and end. The spirits simultaneously captured and released air and acid from one side of their mouth through the other—protecting the island—far from the plastic, putrid wastes of a world upside down whose atomic ghosts threatened to haunt this place once more. The dark reminders of an age long forgotten.

I continued through the brush, past an ancient stairwell, past the crooked limestone walls, the ocean eaves my only companion as the scent of salt coated my nostrils. Heavy with the music of the water, tides pooled at my feet. I smiled, standing in the presence of the infinite, the lonely, where gods die on an island at the center of the universe.

The Myth of the Closet

Falling into the wide mouth of wood, regret, and silvery teeth, I watched the creation of stars like false expectations fill the sky, filtering the night with dim shadows and glittery lies, sprinkled o'er the flat faces of billions who knew nothing else. They were sheep wrapped in flesh and too fearful to leave their metal coffins, but I knew better. Below, a whirling, gnashing maw hungrily licked its lips, waiting for the next person to fall; waiting for me to fall; waiting for me to step from outside that ancient closet door,

falling into

the wide,

mouth of wood,

hinges moaned, unable to keep the bulging masses back, pressed behind me, where below I dared not to look down into the swirling darkness happily prepared to consume what was left of me. Called to the most primal insecurities, I couldn't stop them, millions of them like mindless piles of blood, bone, and unreason, climbing over themselves, beckoned by the music of that horrid monster, falling into

the wide,

mouth of wood.

Dear gods, no.

I was falling into the wide mouth of wood,

bodies over bodies

afraid that I'd be the last one,

to fall into that hideous mouth.

The Myth of the Flood

Smothered by the wrath and ruin of my tears, the cities were eventually swallowed by the myth that was my body. Consumed in a liquescent misery, across the Earth, across the rocks and mountains, across the horizon, so that the world might never forget my unhappiness.

Too late were they to forget me, a mass of salt and dread that filled the worst nightmares and twisted fantasies of men. My unshaped body and useless appendages were never beautiful but only tools for a mad god or vile beast. Too quick were they to forget the wonder imbued within the sparkle and light of my cerulean eyes, limitless and gentle. And how easily I was replaced by the deranged, lustful mass which sought to swallow the world.

Their fictions became my truths. I became all too eager, trapped in rage without depth, without control, without the need for patience to wash away the marble temples and stone villages where so many dreams confided in the privilege of safety and comfort. Crashing without the benefit of warning, my fingers like daggers pierced the muddy earth and rocks, bemoaned over the long, tired years by only the stars, who watched my sorrowful destruction.

Forever ruined, my body covered the world, a desecrated truth remembered only in the myth that was The Flood.

Platz, the King of Nothing

I, too, was afraid of the emptiness. Things had to change. Deep within the darkest moments of my desperate loneliness, the most haunting images cradled me like the neon-mothers and phantom-fathers who paraded in cyber-tatters through the waters and crypts, far into the nethers of the world.

The world was going,

        broken and falling,

                And things were going to change.

Cracked, shattered, exploded, my body fragmented across the crooked insides, no longer the Dead-King feared by billions in nightmares so plentiful, no longer the Shade Unimaginable but withered into a cracked helmet. Locked away in the rock and sullen earth, the jewels were the only stars I ever knew.

My world was going,

        broken and falling,

                And things were going to change,

      for I was the King of Nothing.

Drag, Queen of the Underworld

Sometimes the darkness weighed down on my body until I felt as if I was going to be crushed like another piece of rock and ruin. Strewn across some frozen lake, like Nyx languishing within the endless wastes, dragged underneath a parade of daemons, their ugly little feet trampling through the snow and blood, serving a blissful Master where my soul was trapped, clutched against his armored breast: A lifeless toy.

No, things were going to change,

and I was the Queen of Everything.

There's more to these myths than gardens, damsels, and ancient, ugly men. Stories get old after a few thousand years. Recycled, re-used, burned into the memories of wretched men who think themselves more pretentious than the stars. I'd always wanted to redecorate that awful cave he called a *palace*. The gaudy and grotesque face was enough to twist my guts while inside, as a gaggle of old one-eyed gray witches, wandering souls, and three-headed dogs danced like some gaudy macabre burlesque.

Yes, things were going to change,

because I was the Queen of Everything.

I was light, beauty, and darkness, and he needed me. His reasons were mind-numbing and endless, but one thing was clear: a drag queen had been *abducted* by lackluster forces of darkness, and things were going to change around here.

The Chamber of What-If

Coins, gods, witches, and wicked philosophies mattered not inside the old chambers, where possibilities were limited not by marbled demons but lauded by the clockmakers and time-masters who presided over this den of reason. Self-contained by pillars of syntax from the awfulness of hetero-ever-after or constructs of Fate, I built the walls higher, greater, and stronger than any closet or confine, immune to the seductions of expectation. No labors twelve, snake-women, or fairy-tale contracts here in the chambers but what-if and someday soon.

The Old Ways were ripped apart; thrashed, bent, and twisted forever. Happily, I stood at the edge of the chamber, where new myths and transgressive realities were weaved into star-boned columns of light and thought, upending the ugliness of expectation, filling the holes with hope-to-be and brittle coins, corpses of gods and witches, and finally, the old, dead philosophies; forever buried underneath the Chamber of What-If.

As Fate Would Have It

Gods, it was a horrible job. Through the ages, some thought me to be numerous, others assumed I was the personification of the Fate itself. There was no answer, only that I was trapped betwixt death and light, a cursed caretaker forever doomed to witness that which was always falling, burning, and thriving. Heat-death and chilled-chaos existed simultaneously in the universe, and there I was, floating in the middle of it all.

Spin,

               measure,

                           and cut.

Poetic ramblings feverishly scribbled by someone or some *thing* bemused by my abilities. Perhaps it was something I might've done to a civilization, a god, a monster, or even a galaxy. Time's quite the flexible yarn as I drag onward, mostly bored with infinity, so there's nothing left to do except

Spin,

               measure,

and cut.

Hetero Never-After

No more would I be confined to the dread-musings and broke-back hallucinations conscripted by the whitewashed pantheons who stood in crooked numbers over the crimson-faced worshippers. No more, but soon I'd watch *their* world smolder and hear new beginnings rise from the ash, bubbling, hissing with the crackle of new stars whose spectral radiance would cover the heavens in glitter and gold.

The old, musty temples that stood for untold and countless ages, browned by dirt, mud, and a living putrescence, began to crumble from pillar to pew, revealing the ugliness of the myths that we were tube-fed and pipe-dreamed. The bones of the Old Binaries crippled from the inside out. Fragile and feeble gods were unable to prop up the lies and lecherous infinities spreading through the rhizomatic innards of their temple.

No more, though; no more Old Binaries. No more straight connections from edge to edge as if things were *meant to be*. With the final crunch and clamor of stone and staunch-hearted body tumbling over the rubble, this was *their* end and the beginning of *anOther* mythology.

AUTHOR'S NOTE: THE MYTH OF MYTHOLOGY

By: Maxwell I. Gold

Mythology plays a critical role in the structure of human storytelling. The study of myth, but more closely, it's how we see ourselves through the lens of a particular worldview. There are many ways the old myths from Homer to the Prose Edda convey a heteronormative worldview and perception of what-should-be versus what-could-be. From ruthless and prideful Norse gods who crowed at their bloody victories, praising the toxic idolatry of the hyper-man, to the stories of gods too burdened with sadness that they'd have to resort to transform their mortal or demi-mortal same sex lovers into either flora, fauna, or some anthropomorphic thing – to save themselves from facing their own godly peers, or themselves. We've read all the stories and seen them through their lens.

I wanted to reshape that lens.

No, I wanted to completely break it, because it didn't matter how we as queer people were seen, but it mattered more how we saw ourselves.

The poems in this collection, I hoped, might evoke that sense of wonderment but also through an intersectionality of folklore blended from various cultures including Greek, Okinawan, Tahitian, and many others, create something new and beautiful.

As a queer writer, it was important that these poems echoed a sense of the other by taking those old gods and monsters and pushing them on their heads (or backs). Mythology too, takes us through a place which allows deep, primal truths to flow from both calloused and spiritual places, so close to our hearts like some dark grotto tucked away and secret for thousands of years; where we've discovered the songs that allow us to commune with gods, dance with faeries, and tame even the greatest of monsters.

These are myths that are meant for us. They are no longer the gods and monster of old. They're long dead, and anOther mythology begins, now.

ABOUT THE AUTHOR

Maxwell I. Gold is a Jewish American multiple award nominated author who writes prose poetry and short stories in cosmic horror and weird fiction with half a decade of writing experience. Some of his books include *Oblivion in Flux: A Collection of Cyber Prose* from Crystal Lake Publishing and *Bleeding Rainbows and Other Broken Spectrums* from Hex Publishers. Five-time Rhysling Award nominee, and two-time Pushcart Award nominee, find him at www.thewellsoftheweird.com.

ABOUT THE COVER ARTIST

Dan Sauer is a graphic designer and artist living in Oregon. In 2016, he co-founded (with editor/publisher Obadiah Baird) The Audient Void: A Journal of Weird Fiction and Dark Fantasy, which features his design and illustration work. Since 2017, he has worked extensively on book covers and interior art for Hippocampus Press and other publishers. His art often takes the form of surreal collage and photomontage, as pioneered by artists such as Max Ernst, Wilfried Sätty, J. K. Potter and Harry

O. Morris. In 2020, he launched his own publishing imprint, Jackanapes Press (www.JackanapesPress.com), which is devoted to publishing weird fiction and poetry.

facebook.com/dansauergraphicdesign

INTERSTELLAR FLIGHT PRESS

Interstellar Flight Press is an indie speculative publishing house. We feature innovative works from the best new writers in science fiction and fantasy. In the words of Ursula K. Le Guin, we need "writers who can see alternatives to how we live now, can see through our fear-stricken society and its obsessive technologies to other ways of being, and even imagine real grounds for hope."

Find us online at www.interstellarflightpress.com.

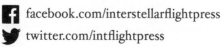

facebook.com/interstellarflightpress
twitter.com/intflightpress
instagram.com/interstellarflightpress
patreon.com/interstellarflightpress

Printed in the USA
CPSIA information can be obtained
at www.ICGtesting.com
LVHW040759060923
757193LV00005B/44